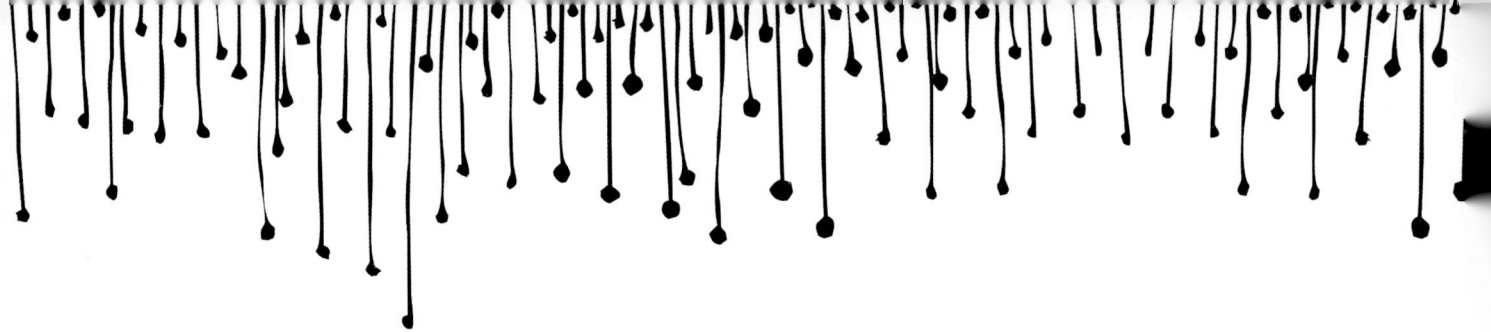

Published by Darf Children's Books
An imprint of Darf Publishers Ltd
277 West End Lane
West Hampstead
London
NW6 1QS

The Dot
By Gulnar Hajo

First published in Arabic by Bright Fingers Publishing House, Damascus, Syria 2014
Originally published as حكاية نقطة على دفتر أبيض (Hekayat Nuqta 'ala dafter abyadh)

Translated by Ruth Ahmedzai Kemp
Edited by Sherif Dhaimish

Storyline and illustrations © 2014 Gulnar Hajo

The moral right of the author has been asserted

All rights reserved

This book is sold subject to the condition that it shall not, by way of trade or otherwise, be lent, resold, hired out, or otherwise circulated without the publisher's prior consent in any form of binding or cover other than that in which it is published and without a similar condition, including this condition, being imposed on the subsequent purchaser.

A catalogue record of this book is available from the British Library.

Printed and bound in Turkey by Elma Basim

ISBN-13: 978-1-85077-329-0

www.darfpublishers.co.uk

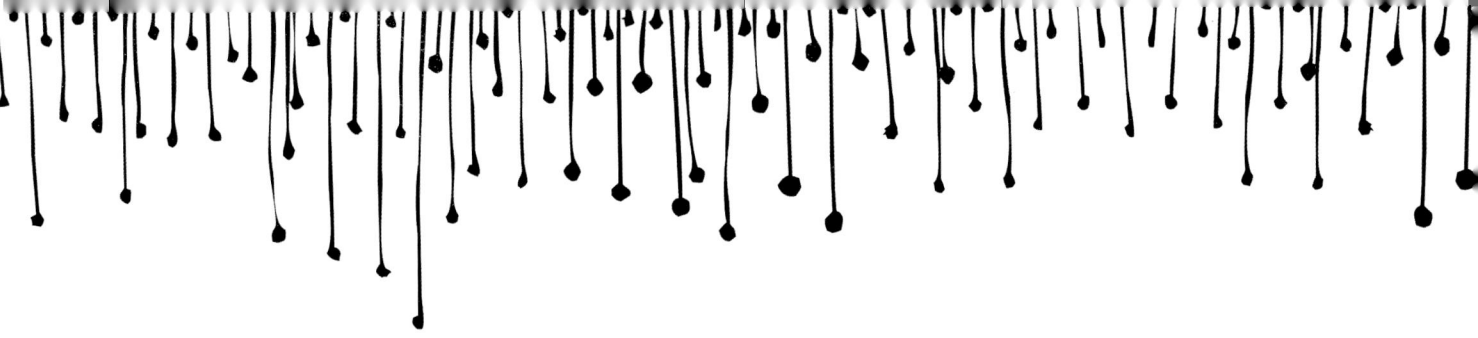

The Dot

by Gulnar Hajo

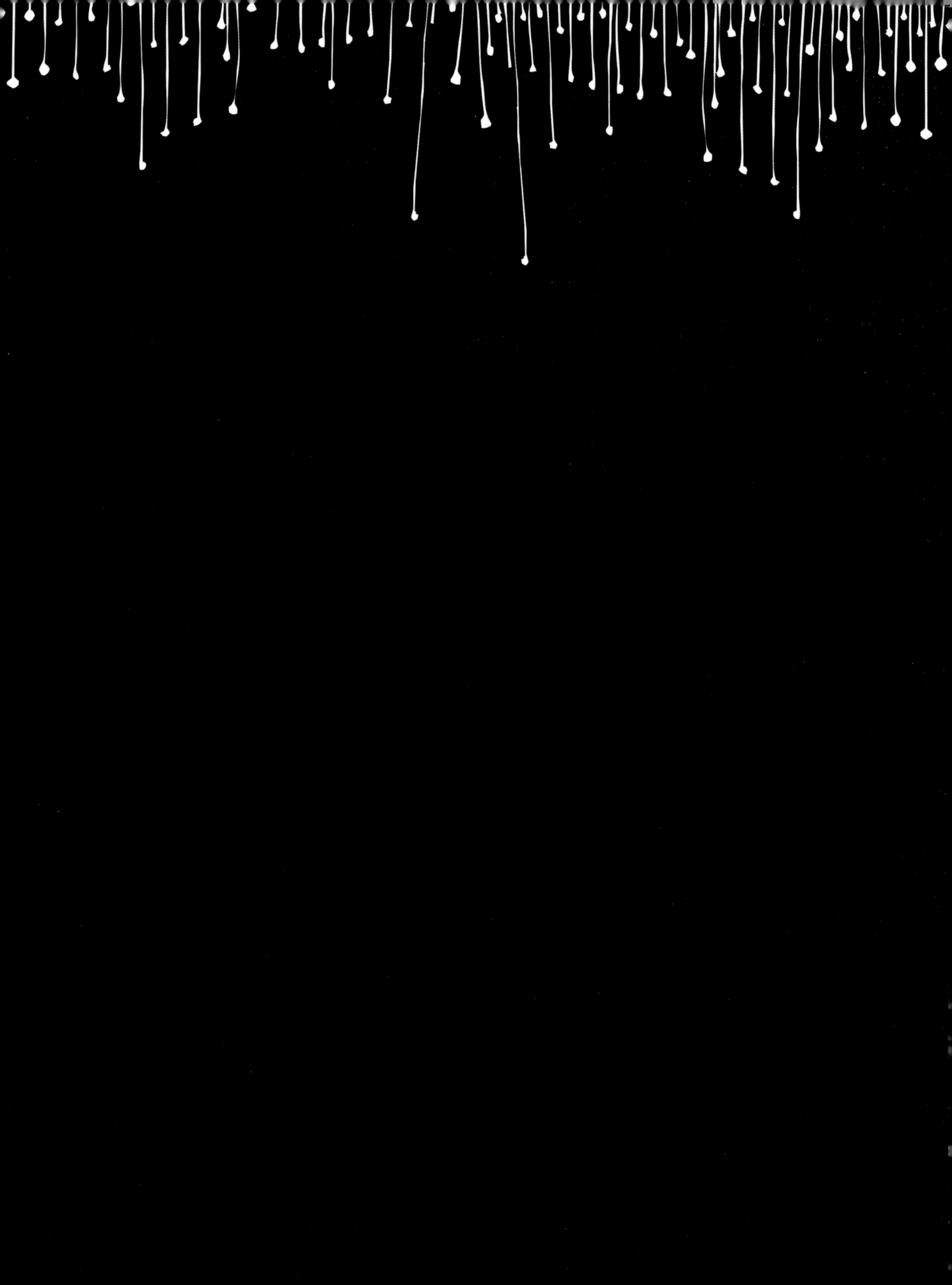

Once upon a time in the big broad universe, there was a dot.

It lived for years and years in the same place at the end of a line.

One day, the dot couldn't sit still any longer.
It went for a walk along the straight line.

When it got bored of walking,
it went back again.

On its way, it found some other dots.
They were also bored of sitting still.

They all decided to do something together.
To make something.

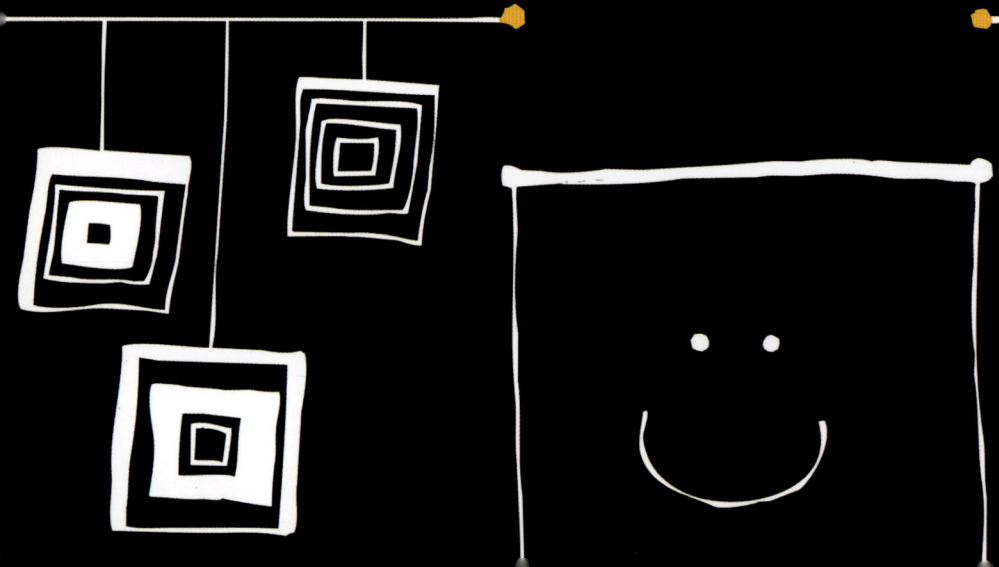

The four dots each walked in a different direction and stopped the same distance apart.

Together they made a square!

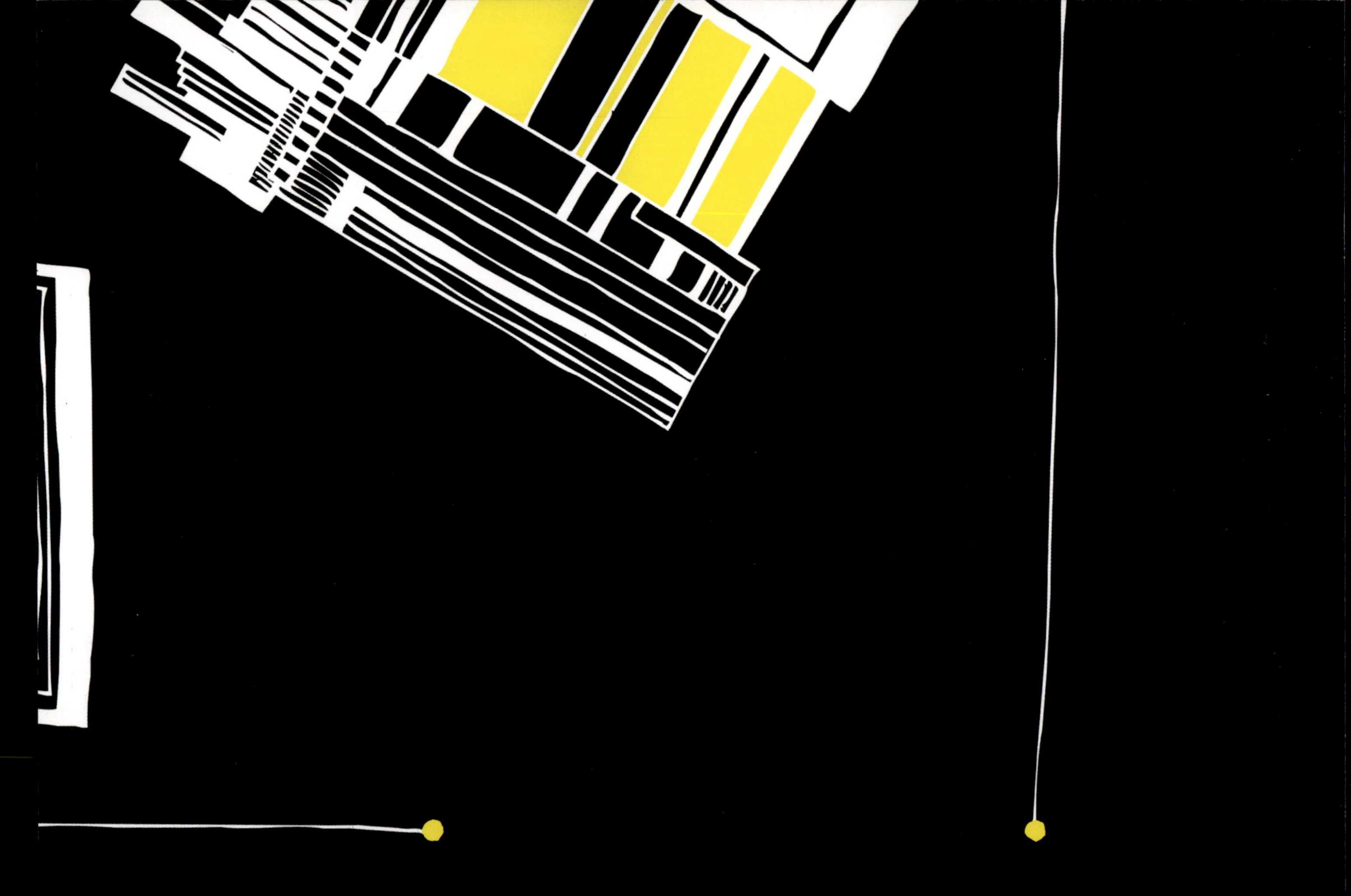

Four more dots heard what was going on.
They wanted to have a go.

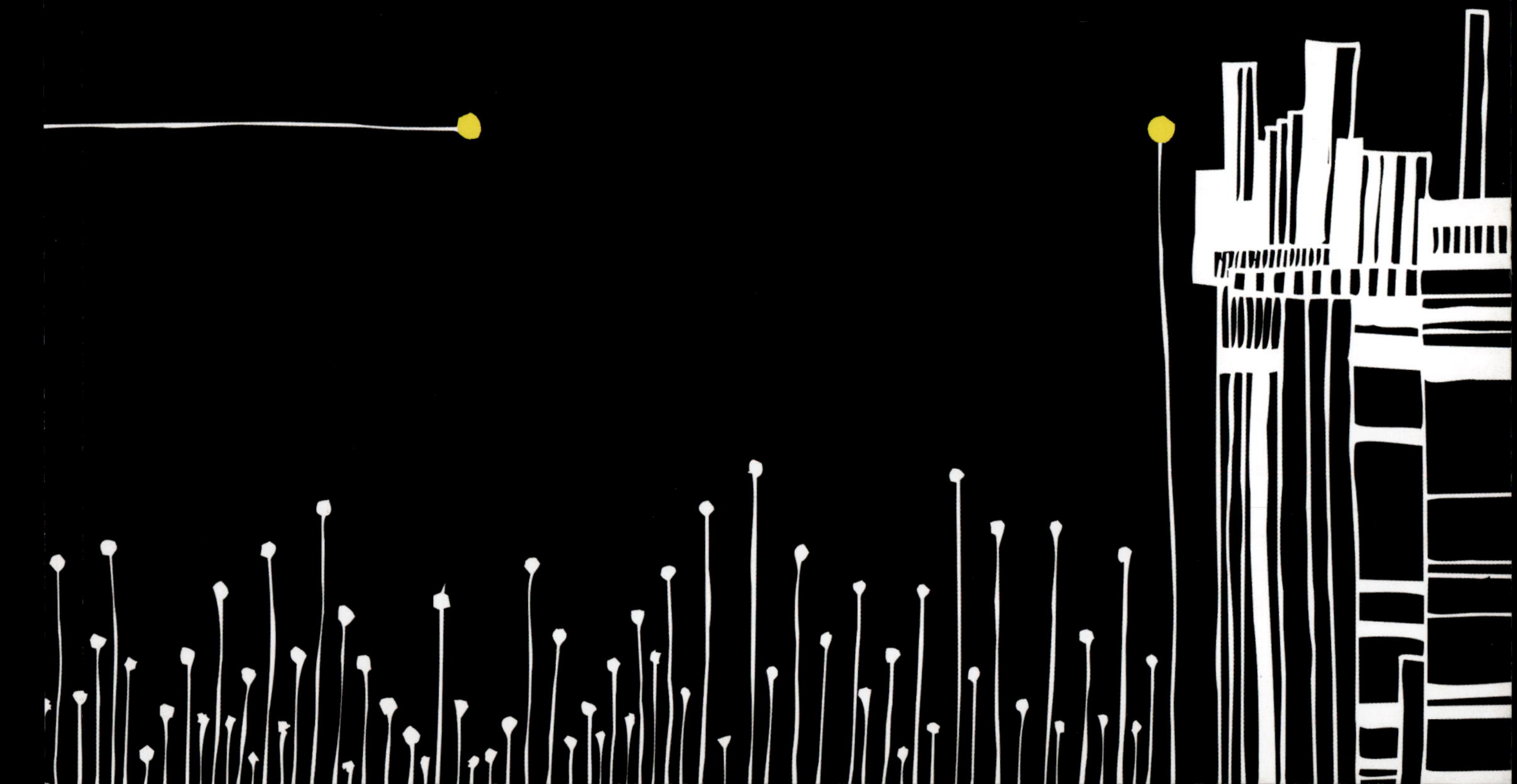

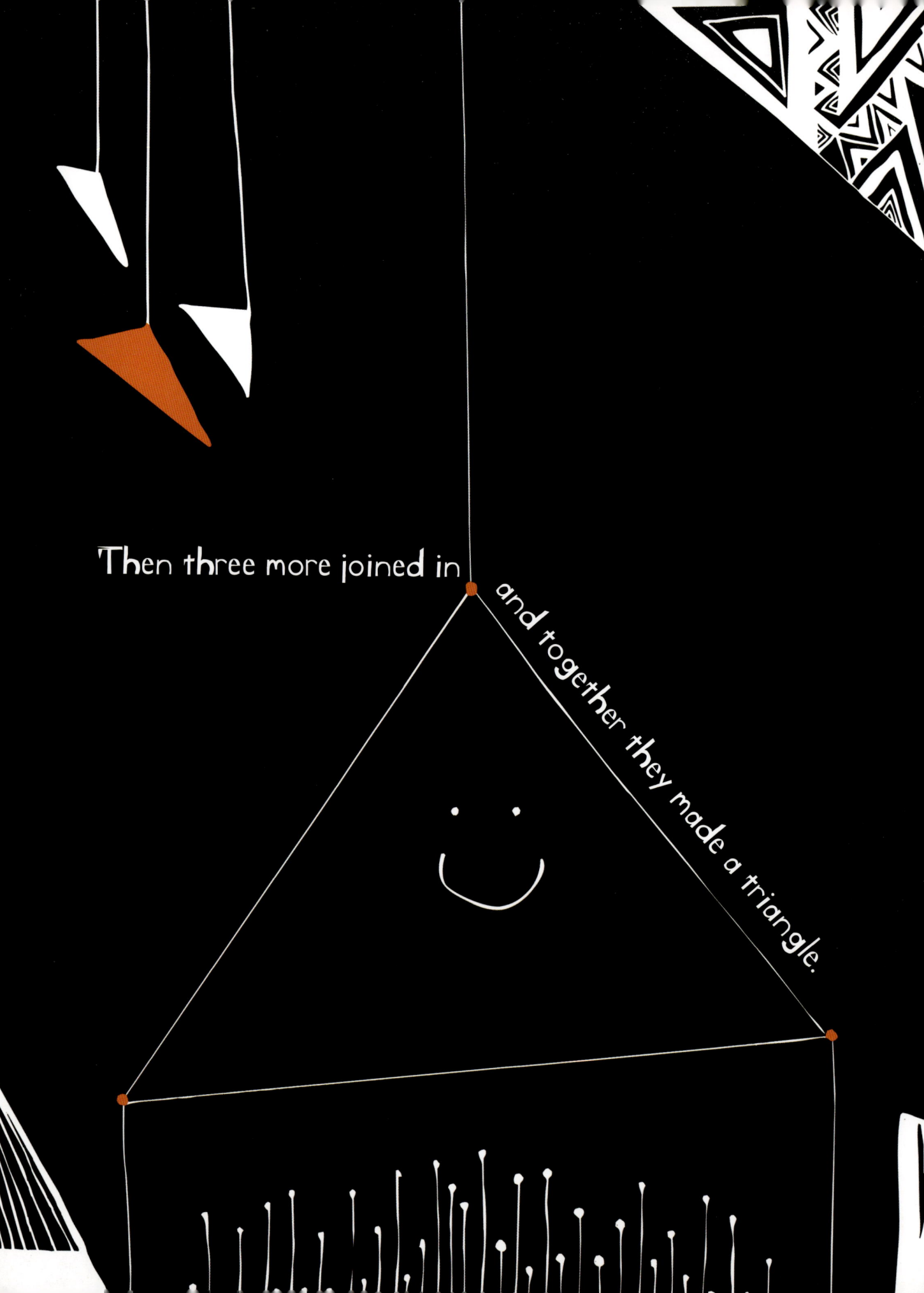

More and more dots hurried over to join the fun.

When one made
a circle,
they all
wanted
to do it.

Soon there were circles everywhere!

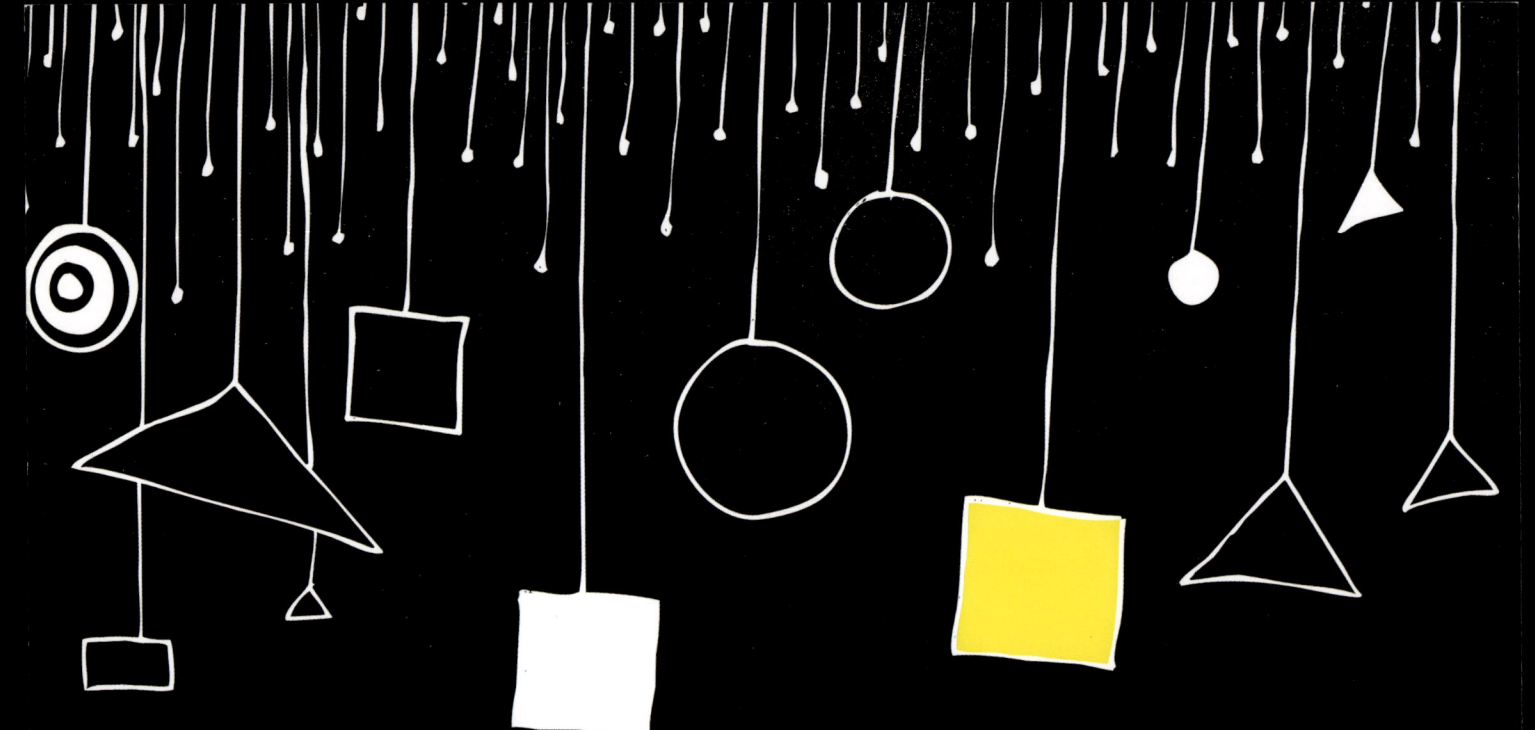

They had made lots of different shapes ...
a rectangle, a square, a triangle and a circle.

Then the square
and the triangle
sat next to each other
and realised they could
make a house.

The shapes were amazed by what they could make if they worked together.

There was no end to the possibilities!

One circle wanted to be a moon to light up the dark sky.

Some lines and shapes made a girl, a boy and a cat, and they all became friends.

The rays from the sun made the world warm and light.

The girl and the boy played in the lovely garden.

And the children, and the cat, went home to sleep.